Mari Pringle has used her life experiences in her writing. She has worked in many different settings since starting work at 15.

Her observations of people in ordinary situations are the foundation of her stories, which were honed in a creative writing class at the "Lit and Phil" in Newcastle-upon-Tyne.

She strives to make her work entertaining and heart-warming, with a colourful cast of unforgettable characters.

Now a retired mum of three and gran of seven, she lives in a village near Durham City. Apart from her writing, her passions are travelling, crochet and her dog, Bobby.

Thanks to all my colleagues I worked with between 1994 and 2005, my inspiration came from our interactions.

Mari Pringle

IT'S ELECTRIC

AUSTIN MACAULEY PUBLISHERS™

LONDON • CAMBRIDGE • NEW YORK • SHARJAH

A CIP catalogue record for this title is available from the British Library.

ISBN 9781398419346 (Paperback)
ISBN 9781398419353 (ePub e-book)

www.austinmacauley.com

First Published 2022
Austin Macauley Publishers Ltd®
1 Canada Square
Canary Wharf
London
E14 5AA

I would like to thank Austin Macauley Publishers for giving me the opportunity to become a published author.

FOR JACKIE,
WITH LOVE,

Mervin Pringle.
x

Chapter 1

Marcus White sighed as he tried to get his fob to open the shutters of the 'It's Electric' superstore.

Why does this always happen to me, he thought. *Especially on bank holiday weekend!*

If the damned shutters won't open, I will have to call an engineer, and inform David Smithson, the area manager, and head office. He will go nuts at the cost, he thought to himself, whilst frantically clicking the open button.

Only recently promoted to assistant manager, Marcus wondered if it was worth it, as he made more money for less hours and less stress as top sales person. Just then, he heard the throaty roar of Jason Doubleday's sports car.

Jason was the other assistant manager.

As it was a bank holiday, all staff had to be in, so they were both there.

"What's up Marcus?" Jason shouted over as he locked the car door. "Have you forgotten your fob again?" he sniggered.

Jason liked to be top dog.

It's Electric's golden boy had risen from being a temporary Christmas warehouse helper, to assistant manager in 18 months. He was ambitious and charming or as Marcus thought, smarmy, and always money-orientated.

Yes, it was a good trait for a sales person, but there was something about it Marcus wasn't sure he liked.

Marcus wanted to be a success in the company himself, but Jason made things jangle in the back of his head.

Suddenly the shutters groaned and started to open, as Jason approached waving his fob and saying, "Did you forget to charge yours on your day off then?"

Marcus sighed again, no he hadn't charged it. It was the first Sunday he had had off in months. Somehow, Jason managed to do a Sunday about every two months, when it was supposed to be alternating week by week between the two of them.

They both entered the store leaving the electric doors partly open and the shutters far enough down so the staff could duck down to get in, but not enough for customers to think they were open.

Snapping the lights on, Marcus gazed around. The store was a mess! Appliances out of place, price tickets missing TVs not wired in etc.

Typical of any morning after Jason's shift, he thought to himself.

"Right Jason," Marcus said, "when the team get in, I will do the target meeting if you ring in your final figures for yesterday."

As they went through the double doors to the staff area and warehouse, yet again there was a mess. Boxes not broken down, a number of kettles and toasters on the stairs leading to the small appliances' stockroom, and a vacuum cleaner standing at the back door.

"Okay, it's coffee time before that lot come in and we can't get near the kettle," Jason said.

"Good idea," Marcus replied, meanwhile thinking he would need a gallon to get through the day!

The staff weren't going to be pleased about clearing up the mess, as some of them hadn't been in the day before.

Just then the door was flung open, and in a rush as usual, Rosie burst in spluttering, "Blooming kids, anyone want three? Why can't they just do what I say the first time? I'm sick of yelling myself hoarse every morning. Maybe I should stop working, that would give them a shock. There would be no mum's taxi, or sports gear then!"

"Morning, Rosie, want a coffee?" Marcus asked.

"Yeah, I would love one, make it strong please, as I'm tired before I start!"

"Were you working at the hotel last night?" Marcus said as he handed her the coffee.

"Yep," Rosie replied. "Mouths to feed, bills to pay, person roll on retirement eh. That's if I haven't gone out in a shower of sparks first."

Marcus felt sorry for Rosie a lot of the time, she always did her job right, never took time off, and he knew she worked like a Trojan in the local hotel bar. *I don't suppose she has much choice,* he mused, *on her own with two teenagers and a four-year-old.*

Although Rosie didn't say much, he knew by shop floor gossip that she had been in a difficult relationship, and had to pack her life into bags one night and leave her home to escape her partner.

Most of the team were starting to arrive in dribs and drabs, some looking a bit worse for wear.

Jonathon Delaney, the youngest member of staff, looked like he had slept in his uniform. He was definitely being a runner in the warehouse today! No customer facing jobs for him looking like that.

Aline and Joan always travelled in together and were like two peas in a pod. They appeared with Jonathon, chipping him about the state he was in.

The other members of staff came in next.

Alice whose behaviour was seen as odd by the others, Sonya who thought herself a cut above the rest, Dave solid as a rock, and Bob who was looking forward to his retirement in the next few months.

"Right," Marcus shouted above the racket, as they were all talking at once. "Grab a coffee and come to the signing up room, it's target-talk time."

Lots of moans and groans were heard.

They all hated TTT, it was also the company's motto: Target the customer, Talk to the customer, Tie up the sale.

It took another five minutes for them to all get into the signing up room. This was where the customers were taken when they wanted finance options, so they had some privacy while entering their details.

Rosie who was the sales admin, was tidying the application sheets while she waited for everyone to settle.

Marcus took a deep breath then said, "Okay you lot, today is bank holiday Monday, lots of customers will be looking for deals. You can offer them 10% yourselves, or come and see me or Jason if you need more to clinch the deal. It's the start of a new week so check your personal targets, you could do well towards that magic number. All you need is the right attitude, and remember TTT!"

"He's absolutely right folks," said a voice from the door.

The shop manager Grant Anderson had arrived.

"Now let's get the doors open and the money rolling in. I'm looking at doing top store this week. Remember my bonus depends on your performance folks."

Just what we all need to hear, thought Rosie to herself, *about your bonus Grant!*

For all that, Rosie liked Grant, he was always fair with the staff unlike other managers she had worked for. In appearance Grant looked like a 1950s film star, with his slicked back hair and well-groomed moustache, but the illusion ended there. He was from a large, industrial town some miles away, and had four kids, two dogs and a demanding wife who kept him on his toes. Hence, the rather battered 4x4 he drove rather than a posh motor, which most other store managers cruised around in.

By this time, everyone was on the shop floor chatting to each other in groups. Sales people always had a lot to say.

Marcus and Jason were behind the counter. From this position they could see the whole floor, though once customers started coming in, they would be on the shop floor driving the sales, whilst Rosie would be behind the counter putting through small sales for the others, leaving them free to get back out there to close that deal.

Some sales people could close deals on packages on TVs, or kitchen equipment easily, costing a lot of money, and bagging themselves a lot of commission, whilst others struggled to sell even a kettle or a toaster. It wasn't a job for the fainthearted.

"Okay folks," Grant shouted across the shop, "let the day begin," as he pressed the door open button on the key pad.

No doubt someone would switch it back to sensor, so it only opened when people went past, as the wind blew straight in most days, and only managerial staff were allowed to wear jackets.

Rosie had taken the precaution of buying two long sleeved thermal vests when she had started the job in September as she hated being cold! It seemed as if her brain froze, and she couldn't function properly when the temperatures dropped.

Marcus called across to Rosie who was chatting to Joan and Aline, "Let's swap places, here come the customers."

"Catch you later girls," Rosie mouthed, and went off behind the counter.

Rosie was at the computer, busy loading some information on to the stores stock control page, when she was suddenly aware of a presence.

Alice was leaning on the counter with both hands. Because it was about 4ft high, she was staring directly at Rosie, who sighed inwardly, whilst smiling at Alice.

"Do you need something Alice?" Rosie asked.

"Can you see anything?" Alice whispered, peering about her.

"Yes," Rosie laughed, "lots of electrical goods!"

"No, no, I mean anything around me?" Alice said, still glancing around.

Alice and Rosie had this conversation on an almost daily basis over the last few weeks, as Alice had overheard Rosie talking to a lady who arranged psychic evenings in local pubs.

One of Rosie's talents was, she was a tarot reader. Usually she kept this to herself, and was regretting the fact she had been overheard, especially by Alice.

"Alice, I've told you every time you have asked, I'm not always in psychic mode, and why are you whispering?" Rosie sighed.

"In case they hear me, you know, the spirits," Alice was still whispering.

"Look Alice, as I've said before, unless I'm doing you an actual reading, I'm not tuned in. Today I'm a sales admin."

This wasn't strictly true, as Rosie often picked things up, but she certainly wasn't letting Alice or any of the others know that!

Blimey, she's like a cross between a character in the Vicar of Dibley, and some horror movie. Rosie laughed to herself.

Just then, Alice spotted a lady looking at the vacuums, and off she shot like a heat-seeking missile, Rosie was convinced customers often bought from Alice just to escape her weirdness.

"That blooming Alice," hissed Aline, "she's got that customer, I was just going over there. Where did she spring from? It's always the same in here. Thank God Jonathon I will do anything for a sale. Delaney is in the warehouse today, or you and me wouldn't stand a chance Joan, I hate it when she's in, don't you!"

Joan nodded in agreement, adding parrot fashion. "I hate it when she's in."

Sonya Glass sailed across the shop floor towards them, "What are you two bitching about now?" she asked, sensing the bad mood Aline was brewing.

"We weren't bitching," Joan replied. "Just stating a fact, no one else can get a sale for Dippy Dinah over there."

"That's a fair point," Sonya agreed, "but you were chatting and missed your chance. Grant is always telling the pair of you at the weekly meetings, so you only have yourselves to blame," and off she sailed again leaving behind a waft of expensive perfume.

"I can't stand that stuck up madam," Aline said as she glared at Sonya's retreating back.

Sonya did see herself as a cut above the rest, as she had worked at an upmarket cosmetic counter in a huge department store, until she had recently moved back North. She did nothing to hide her opinions and it won her no friends.

"Hi there, Rosie," a voice broke into her thoughts as she watched the usual shop floor pantomime unfold. "Any sales on yet?" Bob asked.

He had been helping Jeff, the warehouse man, sort out the mess behind the scenes.

"No, nothing yet, though I think Alice might be scaring that woman into buying a Dyson," Rosie laughed.

"How's Jeff, I haven't had a chance to speak to him yet. There aren't any stock problems are there? I'm pretty sure, looking at the stock control that we are okay after yesterday's back up delivery. It all looks ship shape to me and you know Jeff, he takes it all in his stride and just laughs at everything."

Rosie really liked Jeff. He made her job so much easier. The last warehouse man had been Jeff's complete opposite. Robbie had been bad-tempered, impatient, stubborn and brusque. He always thought he was right, and often had open arguments with the sales staff, which on one occasion had boiled over into fisticuffs. Rosie had to step in between them, whilst yelling for Grant to come down from his office!

Luckily the sales person was only covering for holiday leave, and went back to his own store two days later, but it made the rest of the staff scared to ask Robbie for anything.

Robbie was always moaning about his pay too, so he had gone off to be a doorman at a local night club. *No doubt he would enjoy kicking drunks out, instead of booting the stock about,* Rosie surmised. No more mysteriously dented items for her to try and rid of, having to massively discount them!

At lunch time the store was so busy everyone was only allowed 30 minutes' break. Some of the staff didn't even get that, as their customers came back after checking out the other electrical retailers on the retail Park.

Rosie herself was so busy, she only got time to grab a coffee, and a few bites of her sandwich, as finance agreements had to be verified by her as they came through.

By the time they closed at 4 pm, Rosie was thankful it was an early finish instead of the usual 8 pm! What a busy day it had been. Luckily, all the tills and paperwork balanced. But something was making Rosie feel uneasy, but she couldn't work out why. She was far too tired to start rechecking everything, so she decided to leave it till the morning.

Chapter 2

Rosie was still mulling things over when she got home.

I'm so grateful to my mum, for taking the kids away with her this week, she mused. *I don't think I could cope with a busy shop, and that Sunday shift at the Hotel took the biscuit!* The place had been chock a block full.

Rosie's mother had friends in Whitby, who ran a B&B. She visited them every year at this time, and had suggested to take all three grandchildren with her, as the youngest was now four, and old enough to enjoy it. But also because she worried about Rosie working too hard, and not getting a break.

Coo I'm so tired, as soon as I've eaten this microwave meal, I'm off to bed, Rosie thought. The meal wasn't very appetising, especially as Rosie usually made home-cooked food. But beggars can't be choosers, so she ate it.

All too soon, the alarm went off. Rosie made sure she had enough time in the mornings for a 30 minutes' window, to drink her fresh coffee and gather her thoughts. None of this-leaping-out-of-bed and dashing-straight-out for her.

She let the dogs out in the garden, while she made herself a lunchtime sandwich, and some cheese on toast. Always on a budget, she couldn't afford to indulge in bacon sarnies from the McDonald's on the retail park like the others.

Poor dogs, Rosie thought, *I never have time to take them for a walk, unless it's my day off.* Oh well, they seemed happy enough. Thank goodness the back garden is quite large.

As Rosie drove the few miles to It's Electric, she ran yesterday's big sales through her mind. One of the reasons she had been chosen as sales admin was, Grant knew she had an exceptional memory for people's names and their purchases. He had even rung her for some information when she had taken the kids on holiday! This made Rosie question whether mobile phones were a good idea, but, it was the year 2000, and technology was moving forward.

The day before during the lunchtime breaks, Jonathon Delaney had to go on the shop floor to cover the person having lunch. As usual, and despite his crumpled uniform, he had managed to snaffle a big sale.

Rosie ran her video-like memory back through her head. She could remember the sale. An American fridge-freezer, and the customer's name, which was Gerald Williams.

Hmm, she thought, *the customer definitely passed the finance criteria, but there was still something not right. It had been exceptionally busy, and Jonathon was being more than helpful, not his usual style once the sale was closed.*

Suddenly, Rosie realised what was wrong!

There had been a queue of people waiting for finance deals to go through the checking system. Mr Williams had been quite annoyed at waiting to be checked. As the New Master of one of Durham University's Colleges, he was miffed that he had to go through the same procedure as everyone else. He had made it abundantly clear, by spouting off about how well he was paid, and was a pillar of the community.

She remembered Jonathan trying to placate him, but she also now remembered Jonathon saying, "Just sign here Mr Williams, I will ring you as soon as it goes through, just give me your mobile number. The fridge-freezer will be delivered as soon as there is a slot in your area. It won't be longer than a couple of days."

Oh no, she thought, *I better check that paperwork!*

After any busy weekend, it was Rosie's job to file all the financial agreements. So it wouldn't be noticed that she went straight to her office to check out her suspicions. After a couple of minutes rifling through the paperwork she found the agreement.

Her heart sank. Jonathon had managed to persuade Mr Williams to sign before he had filled in all the final figures. She knew he had refused the insurance, because Jonathon had got her to explain in detail why it was a good idea to purchase it on such an expensive item. Mr Williams had still refused.

But, there it was on the agreement in black and white, the insurance figure. It was only £80 against an £800 item, but it would put Jonathon's figures in the company's top ten for insurance she thought. Sure enough, when she checked the shop system there was Jonathon top of the tree against his sales.

Oh god, Rosie sighed. *How was she going to handle this?* Not only would she have to bring this to Grant's attention to deal with, but also it was fraud. She knew without a doubt that if this came to Mr William's attention he wouldn't be okay with it, or keep it quiet!

Chapter 3

Rosie knocked on Grant's office door.

"If that's you Rosie," Grant shouted, "you better be bearing a cup of coffee."

"I will get you one," she shouted back, and went downstairs to the staff room.

While she waited for the kettle to boil, she wondered how she was going to broach the Jonathon subject, as Grant would be cock a hoop with the figures.

Here goes, she thought, as she went back upstairs with two cups of coffee, as she felt she might need one too.

Pushing the door handle down with her elbow, Rosie went into the room. Grant had the large calculator he favoured and a pile of sales prints in front of him.

He looked up and smiled.

"Wow, Jonathon had a great day yesterday, considering he was in the warehouse for most of it," he said, "I'm starting to wish I hadn't agreed to his transfer to the Brown goods-only store."

Rosie blinked slowly, what did he just say?

"Brown goods-store? Grant, how's this come about?" she queried.

"Well, David Smithson has been looking at everyone's figures, and talking about staff swapping stores to play to their strengths. He thought Jonathon could do well selling all that hi-fi equipment and the larger TVs, plus they are doing a lot more with computers now, and he's PC-savvy. With his charm and sales pitch, he will do well, as he can certainly close a deal." Grant replied.

"I agree with his deal closing being great, but there's something I need to show you, I will just go and get the paperwork from the American fridge-freezer sale before I start," said Rosie buying herself a couple of minutes.

She stepped out the door and round the corner into her own office, leaning against the door as it closed behind her.

How am I going to deal with this one, she wondered. No point in beating about the bush, Rosie decided, as she picked up the financial agreement. *Let's get it over with,* and she headed back to Grant's office.

"I need you to look at this agreement Grant," Rosie said as she handed him the sheets, "as you will see, we still have the customer's copy as he left the store before it passed through the checking system."

"Okay," Grant said slowly, "we can post the customer the copy out though, can't we?"

"Yes, we can," Rosie replied, "but the problem is I heard the customer specifically say he didn't want the insurance."

"But it's on here in black and white," Grant muttered.

"Yep, it is, and that's the problem Grant! Jonathon got the customer to sign, as he wasn't happy waiting, all the figures, except the final set, were on at this point. Jonathon has added the insurance in after the customer signed which is fraud. If Mr Williams sees this, I can guarantee, he won't let sleeping dogs lie. He's a big wig in the university and very self-assured and loud. I can see us and the company in the local news, if we don't sort this out! I can redo the paperwork and take it round for him to re-sign, because we can't alter this now, as it passed with the insurance on it. It will have to be cancelled off and put through again. What's worse is, Jonathon told Mr Williams three or four days for delivery. It's a special order so it will be a week at least, and that's if they are in stock! I've had my suspicions before about some of his sales, massive discounts to get the insurance etc. To be frank, he always forgets the special orders. Lucky for him, I always recheck what he's done as there was a big hoo-hah, which I had to sort out a few months back," Rosie ranted.

"You better send him up here then," Grant said looking deflated, as he could see his bonus disappearing.

Rosie sighed as she went down to the sales floor. She knew three things, she was going to have to sort out this mess. Jonathon would probably bamboozle Grant into believing it was a mistake, and she for one would be glad to see the back of him, when he went to the Brown goods-store.

Chapter 4

"Jonathon, Grant wants to see you in the inner sanctum," Rosie called to Jonathon, who was holding court in the centre of the shop.

The rest of the staff pinged off to various corners like snooker balls as Jonathon moved off.

As she was back on the sales floor, Rosie decided to check the system to see if any sales had gone through. It was usually quiet the day after a bank holiday.

She had just logged on when Aline and Joan appeared at the counter, "So," said Aline, "what's his lordship done now?"

"I'm not sure he's done anything, Grant just wanted to see him," Rosie replied.

"A likely story," the pair chorused, as they walked off laughing like drains.

Marcus was just approaching the counter as he was on late finish and had just come in.

"What's going on Rosie?" he said, "those two shot off at speed, you look fed up, and where is Jonathon, he's meant to be in today."

"Jonathon is with Grant, I'm going to let him fill you in with the latest Delaney debacle when you have your briefing.

I'm off to my office to finish yesterday's paperwork, as I'm only in half day today, thank God," Rosie sighed.

As Marcus was making himself a coffee in the staff room, he saw Jonathon pass the glass door, so he picked up the internal phone and rang Grant's office.

"Is it okay if I pop up?" he asked.

Grant's reply of, "I think you better, as there are a couple of things to go over," made Marcus's heart sink.

Two minutes later, Marcus was sitting in front of Grant's desk.

"Right, the first thing I need to speak to you about is Jonathon."

"Yeah, Rosie told me he was up here when I came in, what's he done now?" questioned Marcus.

"Take a look at this agreement Marcus."

Marcus took the paper and scanned it for mistakes.

"Looks great to me, especially as he's got the insurance on," he said.

Grant sighed as he replied. "Yeah, it looks great, apart from the fact he's up to his old tricks again, getting customers to sign before filling in the final figures. Remember before we employed Rosie, you caught him doing this on that hi-fi? The one the two lads were buying in the sale. The two of them were still wet behind the ears, and Jonathon made a meal of it. Well the trouble is, this time he's picked a university bod! He's the new master at one of the colleges, who will definitely cause trouble if he realises what's happened. Luckily, Rosie and her sixth sense sussed there was something wrong, and found it first thing this morning. Plus he didn't special order it, so let's hope there is one available for delivery, or we are likely to lose the whole sale. I'm just happy I've signed him off to the Brown goods store."

Marcus sat in stunned silence, he thought Jonathon had listened to him, when he was disciplined after the hi-fi sale. Obviously not!

"Well, Graeme Jones won't wear any of his dodgy deals in his store, that's for sure!" Marcus said with conviction.

He knew only too well, what a tight ship the Brown goods store was, as he had started his career their as weekend staff.

Grant picked up the phone.

"I've got to ring David Smithson to confirm I've transferred dodgy Delaney, so will you cancel and reapply the sale to the finance system without the insurance. Then give the new paperwork to Rosie. She's already agreed to go to the customer's house to get him to re-sign. Though exactly how she is going to get him to agree to it, I've no idea. Good job she's a people person eh!"

"Will do Grant," Marcus said as he got up, and went off to look for Rosie.

Chapter 5

Rosie was sitting in her office behind a mountain of paperwork!

Generally, they had done well against the shop's target, which was good news for everyone, and Rosie was making steady progress through the pile.

"Hi, just me," said Marcus knocking, and stepping through the door in one move.

"I guess Grant's updated you on the latest with Jonathon. Just don't let Graeme know his nickname is Dodgy Delaney till after he's gone," she laughed.

"Don't worry, I won't," Marcus grinned back.

He had no doubt that this nickname was one of Rosie's concoctions.

"I have to cancel and redo this agreement. Grant said you were going to deal with the customer, but if you don't want to, I'll go instead," Marcus suggested.

"No, it's okay, Marcus, as Mr Williams, or professor should I say, has already met me, so he may be more amenable, or that's what I'm hoping. I'm going to ring and check if he's in first though. You go and re-input the data. At least there shouldn't be a queue today. Some were taking an hour to go through yesterday. Here goes," she said picking up the phone.

A few minutes later Rosie appeared at the signing up room door.

"It's gone straight through, no bother," Marcus said waving the new agreement at her.

"Great, I've just spoken to Mrs Williams and he's due in for lunch at 1 pm. It's 12:30 now, so I will dash up there. Will you tell Grant where I've gone please? I'm just going to grab my bag and car keys," and with that Rosie shot back upstairs.

A couple of minutes later, Joan and Aline watched her grab the agreement off the counter, and scoot out the door.

"Wonder where she is off to in such a hurry, I thought we weren't supposed to take agreements out of the store, I'm going to find out what's going on," Joan said to Aline, and she headed off to speak to Marcus who was behind the counter. "I thought we weren't allowed to take agreements out of the store. Seems like there's one law in here for us and one for others," Joan remarked.

"Come on, Joan," Marcus replied, "you know that's not true, and Rosie is doing a favour for me and Grant, and it's not up for discussion Joan, so forget it. Some of us have work to do, and there are customers over there at the small appliances, so that's where you should be too," Marcus instructed.

Joan wasn't happy at all being told what to do by a young whipper snapper, even if he was the boss.

She stormed off hissing at Aline as she went past, "I will find out what's been going on."

Chapter 6

Rosie jumped into her car putting the agreement and her bag on the passenger seat.

I hope Mr Williams isn't going to cause a fuss over this, she thought, *I'm meant to be finishing at two today, though it will only take 20 minutes to drive there and back, and the traffic should be light today.*

A short while later, Rosie pulled up in front of a very large 1960's style house, which was tucked away at the end of a short, sweeping drive.

I would never have known this was here driving past, she thought. The house had a very imposing look, all sharp angles and a lot of glass. It was how she imagined a Swedish house to look.

Rosie rang the doorbell; hearing footsteps approaching, she stepped back slightly.

Mrs Williams opened the door and then called over her shoulder, "Gerald the electrical girl is here."

"Do come in, just wait here, he will be with you in five minutes."

Wow, what a house, Rosie thought, with its wide hall, highly polished floor and minimalist furniture it was stunning!

Accompanied by the skittering claws of a well-rounded chocolate Labrador, Gerald Williams approached her wagging his finger.

"Now young lady, what's all this? My wife tells me the paperwork needs resigning. Why's that?"

Luckily for Rosie she was good at thinking on her feet.

"Well Jonathon made a mistake and we aren't allowed to cross out or change anything, so the form had to be redone."

Gerald Williams was staring quite hard at Rosie, "And what mistake was that?" he enquired.

"The figures were back to front, as Jonathon had done it in a bit of a rush," Rosie replied.

"So when is my delivery then?" Mr Williams said.

Rosie knew Mr Williams would ask so she made sure the fridge-freezer was ordered before she left the store.

"It's due here on Monday morning, between 9 and 11 Mr Williams, the delivery guys will ring you en-route and take away all the packing when it's in place, but you need to leave it for about four hours for the gas to settle before switching it on."

It was obvious to Rosie that Mr Williams didn't believe a word of her explanation. Sometimes having a sixth sense was more of a hindrance than a help.

"Your salesperson said a couple of days, not a week from ordering, I can't say I'm impressed by this," Mr Williams said brusquely. "Where do I sign?"

"Just here sir," Rosie indicated the bottom of the agreement, "and this is yours," as she handed him his customer copy.

"I must dash now, if that's okay Mr Williams and thank you very much," Mr Williams fixed upon her with his steely gaze and opened the door.

"Make sure you keep an eye on that young man, or you could be storing up trouble, I've met his sort before." Mr Williams harrumphed and shut the door behind her.

Phew, Rosie breathed out as she got to the end of the drive, *I'm glad that's over.*

"Well done, Rosie," Marcus congratulated her, as she handed him the new signed agreement. "I assume you're off now, as it's your half day."

"Yep I certainly am," Rosie said. "See you tomorrow guys," she called to the other staff as she left the shop.

Joan shot a glance at Aline.

"There's definitely something not right going on there. I've said it before, and I will say it again. I will find out what it is, or my name's not Joan Baxter," she glowered.

Chapter 7

Marcus gazed out over the shop floor and sighed as once again Joan and Aline were standing together.

It's like they are joined at the hip, he thought. *I better go and split them up before Grant comes down.*

As he approached them, Aline said quietly, "Here's your chance Joan."

"Right, ladies, let's have you two at opposite ends of the store please, or Grant's going to be on the war path."

"Oh, is he, but it's okay for people to be coming and going with agreements, and then swanning off on their half day though! As I've said before, one law for us and one for others," Joan spat.

"Look Joan," sighed Marcus, "I've told you before, it's not up for discussion. We had a managerial admin problem and Rosie assisted us in sorting it out, as she should, seeing as she's the admin. What you need to be concentrating on is your figures especially as it's tri-monthly assessments coming up."

"What are you trying to say?" Joan snapped. "I'm not past my sell-by-date yet you know. I can sell as well as any of the others if I get a chance between Dodgy Delaney and that nutcase Alice."

"I'm not saying anything, or implying anything Joan," Marcus replied, "but standing here arguing with me isn't helping your sales."

At this Joan shot him a look of pure venom and stalked off towards a customer who had just walked in.

Marcus glanced at Aline.

"I'm saying nothing," she said, which Marcus knew was exactly the opposite of what she was really doing behind his back.

God this is going to be a long shift with those two. Especially when Joan's in a mood. Why does it always happen when Jason has his day off. His heart sank, as once again he noticed Joan and Aline had their heads together, and what's more Joan hadn't sold the customer anything!

Why did I ever want this job, I can't even remember now, he mused.

"What did he say when I walked away?" Joan asked Aline.

"Nothing," Aline replied, "but look at his face, it's like a wet weekend in Blackpool."

"I'm sure this has something to do with Jonathon," Joan speculated, "in fact I would put money on it."

Just then the door's slid open and in walked David Smithson. Joan and Aline quickly moved apart. As an area manager, Smithson would not stand for any shop floor chatting. You were here to work!

"Morning ladies," he said as he went past.

Luckily Marcus had spotted him, as he pulled up outside the store, and had quickly rang Grant to warn him he was on his way.

As soon as he went through the double doors to the warehouse Joan and Aline moved towards each other.

"There's definitely something going on," Joan whispered. "Otherwise why is he here, when he was only here last week?"

"Morning David," Grant said as Smithson stepped into his office. "Have you come to finalise Jonathon's transfer?"

"I most certainly have," Smithson replied. "Mainly because we want him on board by tomorrow. There are two on holiday on Saturday, so it will leave Graeme short staffed, and as my Jewel in the Crown, it has to have enough bodies hungry for sales. You will have to have both Jason and Marcus in together to boost sales, till I decide whether I'm reshuffling staff again or if you need to start interviewing."

Grant knew that the Brown goods stores would always be at the top of David Smithson's priorities, as it was the background he came from. He had been the manager of a top performing store with an American based company before coming to It's Electric.

"Get Jonathon up here now Grant, he needs to know his last shift here is today, plus I want to prime him on what both Graeme and I expect."

Grant rang the warehouse as Jonathon was helping Jeff clear up so it was ready for tomorrow's delivery.

"Jeff, send Jonathon up," Grant said when Jeff picked up the phone.

Jonathon took the stairs two at a time and entered Grant's office.

"Jonathon," David Smithson said extending his hand to shake Jonathon's. "I'm here to sign your transfer today as I want you to join Graeme's team tomorrow morning."

"No problem, David, I'm raring to go," Jonathon replied. "Not that I haven't enjoyed working here. Grant's a great boss."

"Just remember Jonathon, Graeme likes punctuality and you must be presentable," David told him whilst eyeing his somewhat scuffed shoes. "You better get some black shoe polish when you leave here. If you go looking like that, Graeme will send you home, and you don't want to blot your copy book on the first day, or lose a day's wages now, do you?" he suggested.

"Don't worry David I will go to the supermarket on the way home. They will be super shiny by the time I've finished polishing them," Jonathon replied, flashing David one of his dazzling smiles.

"Right, I must go and check Graeme's got everything in place now, you can get back to whatever you were doing Jonathon, and Grant, I will let you know my final decision on staffing in the next few days. Bye for now," Smithson said, grabbing his briefcase and dashing down the stairs.

"Bye David," Grant called to his retreating back.

"Go on then Jonathon, back to work, and don't stir up that lot on the shop floor when you tell them you are going," Grant said, knowing that the situation was going to cause a river of mischief among the remaining staff.

"So what's the craic then, Jonathon?" Jeff asked.

"I'm off to Graeme Jones's Brown goods store in the morning, so it's my last shift here today," Jonathon chortled!

"Obviously happy to leave us then," the acidic voice of Joan Baxter broke into the conversation as she stepped out of the staff room.

"Oh, hi Joan, didn't see you there," Jonathon replied.

"Is that meant to mean you weren't supposed to let us minions know you're going, because we are always the last to know anything?" she questioned.

"No doubt Grant will be telling us all shortly," Jeff interjected, "and right now I need Jonathon to get off cloud 9 and start helping me sort this place out."

Joan glared at Jeff, snorted, and stalked off back to the shop floor.

"Well, that's her on the war path again. I'm glad I'm in here and not on the shop floor," Jeff observed as he and Jonathon started moving the washers.

Chapter 8

"Blimey Joan, lost a pound and found a sixpence," Dave Johnson chipped Joan, as she came back onto the shop floor looking like a thunder cloud.

"Have you heard then?" she shot at him.

"What are you talking about Joan?" Dave asked. "This sounds ominous."

"Well, Jonathon's been transferred to Graeme Jones store and leaves here tonight. It would have been nice to have been told!" Joan grumbled.

"Ah that's why David Smithson was leaving as I came in," Dave replied, "I thought it was strange him being here twice in two weeks."

By this time Aline had also joined the conversation.

"You and I are off at four, so Grant better get us told before we leave, or I'm not letting sleeping dogs lie. I bet Rosie knows though. She who can do no wrong!"

Dave let out an exasperated sigh.

"Now look you two, let's not start a vendetta against Rosie, she's in the same position as us, just one of the team, not management."

Both Joan and Aline looked down their noses at Dave.

"She's aptly named," Aline spouted. "Cause she always comes up smelling of roses!"

"Yes exactly that." Joan spat.

Luckily at that point a few customers came in making the group disperse.

At ten to four, Grant made his way onto the shop floor. He wasn't looking forward to this chat with his staff at all.

Dave was standing at the TV Display as Grant came through the door, so he motioned him over and asked him to get Joan and Aline to go to the signing up room.

"Right ladies, this won't take very long," he said as they came in. "As you are aware David Smithson came in today and the reason for this was to sign the final papers for Jonathon's transfer to Graeme Jones store. This is his last shift here, so as you two are off home at 4 you can say cheerio when you get your coats as he is in the warehouse with Jeff, that's it, so you might as well go now. I will see you both tomorrow."

"No, you won't," Joan said, "it's our day off, we aren't in till Friday, so see you then," and off they both went, noses in the air.

"Jonathon," they both carolled as they stood at the staff room door, "we've been told to say goodbye."

"Yeah, bye ladies," Jonathon said as he approached, pecking them both on the cheek, then he went back to helping Jeff with a cheery wave.

"Humph, it's all right for some," Joan said in an undertone to Aline, as they walked through the double doors and out through the shop.

"Bye ladies," Marcus called from the counter, "enjoy your days off."

It's like a dark cloud has lifted now those two have gone, he thought to himself.

As Joan and Aline got into Joan's car, they saw Sonya Glass arriving. As usual she looked like a fashion plate, even in her uniform. She was always perfectly coiffed and made up. They both exchanged a look, and Joan drove off.

Grant was still on the shop floor as he was waiting for Sonya to arrive. He motioned for her to come over to the middle of the shop floor where he was standing.

"Hi Sonya, I just need to update you with what has happened today. This is Jonathon's last shift as he is going to work at Graeme Jones store as of tomorrow morning. He's helping Jeff till 5, so you can say cheerio when you go to the staff room."

"Ooh," Sonya replied. "Go Jonathon, I bet that's put some peoples noses out of joint, but it leaves more big sales for me eh." She gave Grant a supercilious grin and walked away.

Grant just shook his head. "Sales people," he muttered to himself.

Chapter 9

A couple of weeks later, after some initial sniping about Jonathon's move, and some panic, as a memo had come round from David Smithson about his plans for putting staff where they would perform best, once again Marcus was opening up.

It was his intention to get the shop ship shape as it was a Tuesday, and generally a quiet day.

Just then Rosie arrived, "Hi Marcus," she smiled.

Marcus pressed his fob and the shutters slowly opened. Both he and Rosie ducked down and pushed the electric doors open to enter the store.

As he expected, Marcus saw the store was a mess again. He sighed inwardly as he said to Rosie, "Well here we go again, another day another dollar."

"Yep," she replied, "it's the only way to keep going eh, focus on our pay, ha-ha."

They went through the double doors to the warehouse. Marcus thought he saw someone on the stairs near Grant's office.

He stopped and tapped Rosie on the arm, "Did you see someone on the stairs there?"

Rosie shook her head, "No, I didn't. Why? Did you think somebody was there?"

What Rosie didn't say to Marcus was, she had often seen a ghostly figure on the stairs and passing the inner window in the staff room. She kept quiet about her abilities to see spirit people and about the insights to situations she often got.

Lately, she had been feeling slightly perturbed about Jason Doubleday, the other assistant manager. She couldn't put her finger on it, but something was amiss.

"I'm just going to check your office and Grant's, plus the backdoors," Marcus said, and off he shot up the stairs.

Rosie went onto the staff room and filled the kettle and washed two mugs. The sink was piled high as usual, though everyone was supposed to wash their own dirty dishes. It was a point she was going to have to get Grant to raise at the weekly meeting.

I better print and laminate some reminders to stick on the wall plus memos for everyone, she thought to herself.

She was just putting the coffee in the cups when Marcus came in looking puzzled.

"Rosie, will you do a stock check on the Dysons please, there's another one at the back door. It looks like a return as it's been used, but they hardly ever go wrong, and this is the second in just two or three weeks. Will you check the returns and repair paperwork too?"

At this point Rosie's heart started racing, which for her was a sign that something was afoot!

Everyone on the morning shift started trickling in, all intent on getting their morning tea or coffee before Target Talk Time!

Marcus had told Rosie not to mention the Dyson to anyone till they had time to investigate further.

During TTT Marcus told the staff they would have to put their own sales through, as he had jobs for Rosie to do in her office. Because it was usually a quiet day there was no complaining from the sales staff about Rosie not putting their sales through the system.

Rosie knew it was going to take a long time to double check all the paperwork and search through the sales, but she was good at the task in hand, and was certain if there were any discrepancies, she would find them.

About two hours later, after a lot of cross matching of sales and deliveries, Rosie realised that not one but two Dysons had disappeared over the last month. There was no repair paperwork either, nor for the one at the back door.

Okay, Rosie thought to herself, *if it's a repair someone could have made a mistake and forgotten to do the paperwork, but yesterday didn't look busy so that probably wasn't the case.*

After a little more detective work Rosie realised that all the Dysons in the last two months had been ordered by and loaded onto the system by Jason.

Usually, on delivery into the store, it was Jeff the warehouse man who loaded them on.

I think I better have a word with Marcus, Rosie decided.

Rosie rang down to the shop floor and asked Marcus to pop up.

"You're not going to like this," she said as Marcus appeared through the door.

"So what's up then Rosie you look a bit concerned."

"Have a look at these orders and deliveries, they have all been done by Jason in the last two months and uploaded by him too. It's a bit strange as normally Jeff does this."

"Hmm, that's weird." Marcus mused.

"Check Jeff's days off on the rota Rosie."

Rosie went to get the paperwork from Grant's office and as she did her heart started its familiar drumming so she knew something was about to transpire.

She took the rotas back to her office, and as they looked at them Rosie knew what was happening but needed Marcus to realise for himself.

Marcus slowly raised his eyes from the rotas and looked at Rosie.

"Do you see what I see here?" he asked.

"Yes I do," was Rosie's reluctant reply.

Grant the store manager had been on holiday when the last three months rotas had been issued, and Jason had been in charge of that.

When Marcus and Rosie looked at the print outs it was obvious that Jeff's days off were only when Jason was in, and the dates matched the Dyson delivery dates.

The Dyson was the most expensive vacuum the store carried, and were worth over £200!

It was also clear that the delivery dates were also when both Marcus and Rosie were on days off.

"Oh crikey Rosie what are we going to do?" Marcus sighed.

Although Marcus wasn't that keen on Jason, he always felt like the staff were like a second family. This was something as a company that It's Electric encouraged as it helped stores to perform well.

"We are going to have to tell Grant," Rosie said.

"Yes, unfortunately we are," Marcus replied, "he's due in shortly, so I will let him know as soon as he comes in. I always had a funny feeling about Jason. I'm turning into you Rosie," Marcus laughed.

Grant's face said it all when Marcus told him about what he and Rosie had uncovered.

"I will inform the security team and let them sort this out," Grant said, "this is far too complicated for us to deal with as a store, and I need you and Rosie to say absolutely nothing to anyone till this gets sorted out."

Neither Marcus or Rosie were sure how they were going to be able to face Jason and behave as if they knew nothing, but, it had to be done.

Chapter 10

The day by day running of the store seemed to go like clockwork for a few weeks. No major hitches and no staff arguments–which was unusual.

Till one day, Rosie was on a late shift.

As she entered the store it felt as if the air was quivering.

Marcus was standing in the meet and greet position at the front of the store, he stepped forward and said, "Be prepared. Jason is upstairs in Grant's office with an investigator from security. It's all kicking off. Apparently, they have photographic evidence as well as a paper trail."

"Oh dear," Rosie replied. "I feel sick."

She moved off, passing by Joan and Aline who as usual had their heads together. *Those two will be dancing a jig once this gets out,* she thought. Rosie took her coat off in the staff room, then went onto the shop floor, as she could hear raised voices in Grant's office.

She started doing her usual checks on the sales for the day, when the double doors burst open and Jason sailed through closely followed by Grant and the security guy, shouting over his shoulder, "You will be hearing from my solicitor."

Marcus who was across the sales floor shot a look at Rosie, and Joan and Aline's eyes almost popped out of their heads.

They heard the roar of Jason's car as he shot out of the carpark at breakneck speed.

Grant and the security guy exchanged a few words, then he left.

Luckily the store wasn't busy as Grant waved them all into the signing up room.

"Okay, folks," he said, "as you can see Jason has left under a bit of a cloud today. He's been caught stealing Dysons and reselling them, so as from today there will only be Marcus and myself till David Smithson sorts something out. Do not talk about this outside as it's classified information. Aline, Joan, do you hear me? I'm going back to the inner sanctum and I don't want any interruptions," and with that parting comment he left the shop floor.

Joan was spluttering, "Did he have to say that to me and Aline, what about everyone else?"

Chapter 11

Eventually after three weeks of temporary people filling in Jason's vacant position of assistant manager, and Marcus having to do extra shifts, the day came for the interviews.

The staff were all abuzz, and they started speculating about who that might be, and who was going to arrive.

Sonya Glass had applied so was already there primping and preening as usual.

Rosie had been instructed by Grant to take the candidates on arrival to the staff room and to point out the loos etc., and make them feel comfortable.

This included Paul Hardcastle from Teesside Park, Brendan Murphy from Team Valley Brown Goods, Janice Webster from Team Valley White Goods, Sue Goodall from Sunderland and of course Sonya Glass.

Of them all Rosie was hoping Sonya didn't get the post as she was already unbearable and she wasn't even senior sales yet!

Paul Hardcastle was the first to arrive, and though Rosie had spoken to him many times they had never met, so it was nice to put a face to a name and a voice.

Paul was tall and blonde and looked nothing like Rosie had imagined.

One by one they came and went and eventually it was Sonya's turn.

She had gone a bit overboard with the makeup Rosie thought, and she suspected her perfume would set Grant's allergies off.

After 30 minutes Sonya came back onto the shop floor, sailed over to Rosie and said, "Grant wants you in the inner sanctum."

"Okay," Rosie replied, "how did it go?"

"I think I did really well, but who knows?" Sonya said.

Rosie headed off upstairs to see Grant, getting him a cup of coffee en-route.

"Ah Rosie, and bearing gifts too," smiled Grant. "I'm glad that's over, and have you any antihistamines on you, Sonya and her blasted perfume has set my allergies off," and suddenly he started sneezing explosively.

"Yep, I always carry them, I will go and get you one," Rosie replied.

As Rosie went into the staff room for the antihistamines, Joan and Aline were on their break and immediately began asking who had got the job.

"I don't know yet," Rosie said going back out and taking the stairs to Grant's office.

"I bet she does know." Joan hissed.

"Yes, I bet she does know," echoed Aline.

"You're a treasure Rosie," Grant said as she passed him the antihistamines.

"I've made a decision, it's going to be Sue Goodall, she's a good all-rounder with both white and brown goods experience and has been senior sales since It's Electric opened in Sunderland, plus she has been acting assistant manager in her own store, and produced good results. I'm going to email them all now and can you print off some letters and send them first class? I will tell this lot before we close or we will get no peace at all, will we?"

"Absolutely not," Rosie replied. "I've already had the third degree from Joan and Aline."

"Okay, I will go down to the shop floor now as those two are due off at 4 and it's 3:45 now," Grant said extracting himself from his chair.

Rosie followed Grant downstairs and onto the shop floor. Sonya's shift had finished at 2 pm, so she would get the email and letter the same as the other candidates.

"Gather around everyone," Grant called across the shop floor.

Blimey I've never seen Joan and Aline move that quick before, Rosie thought to herself as they rushed over.

"Right, everyone, I have made a decision, our new assistant manager is Sue Goodall from Sunderland. She will be starting on Monday and working closely with Marcus for the first couple of weeks till she feels her feet, and let's be welcoming to her, and no sniping at Sonya please," he said pointedly looking at Joan and Aline. "So let's get on and TTT, folks," and with this parting comment he went back to his office.

Joan was glowering at his retreating back, "Humph!!I'll give him TTT," she said as she and Aline went to get their coats.

Later that evening as Marcus and Rosie were closing down the tills and balancing the day's sales, Marcus said to Rosie, "Well off we go to a new era on Monday, I wonder how it's going to go with a woman assistant manager, there's never been one here before."

"There's a first time for everything Marcus, that's us done for today, and I do believe it's home-time," Rosie smiled.

Chapter 12

When Sue Goodall's alarm went off, she wasn't sure she wanted to get up, as sleep had evaded her that night.

Sue hadn't been able to switch her brain off, as today was her first day as assistant manager at the Durham store, and although it was a post she could perform without a qualm, she still felt either nervous or excited, and right now she couldn't decide which.

The store she had said her final goodbye to the day before – she had worked at for the last five years since it opened.

It was on a retail park near her home in Seaham.

Out of town shopping was the new thing. The previous town centre store she had worked at closed its doors and was now student accommodation, having been turned into flats.

It was a beautiful, old Victorian building, a huge department store in its heyday, then split into retail units, and now flats. She sighed as her mind travelled back to sitting on the bus to town, when she first started working there in the 1980's, as a sales person. She hadn't passed her driving test back then.

Now it was 15 years down the line and at last she was making progress, from sales assistant to assistant manager!

Being a woman in electrical retail hadn't been easy, and in fact still wasn't, she mused.

After another glance at the clock, Sue slid out of bed taking care not to wake her husband who was working 2 till 10 shifts at a crisp factory, a few miles away.

Although Sue and Eddie had been married for over 10 years, it was still just the two of them, as they couldn't afford the exorbitant fees to have the treatment they needed for them to have a child of their own, and it wasn't an option on the NHS.

They had accepted the situation a few years before after much heartache, and now were happy to spoil the nephews and nieces from both sides of the family.

Thirty minutes later, Sue looking immaculate in her uniform, she jumped into her white Fiat 500 and sped off. *At least this drive to the store gives me time to plan a bit,* Sue thought as she headed towards the main road to Durham.

Sue pulled into the carpark just as Marcus was parking up.

"Hi there Sue," Marcus said greeting her with a smile. "Ready for this are we?"

"As ready as I can be," Sue replied returning his smile.

Marcus clicked his fob and the shutters started to move. They ducked down and opened the electric sliding doors and entered the store, which was in darkness.

"Just wait there, I will get the lights Sue, till you know where they are," Marcus advised.

"No problem." Sue answered.

She was quite happy to wait, as it was actually pitch black, the only light coming from the gap they had ducked through.

There was a click, a buzzing sound then the lights started coming to life making a pinging noise as they lit up.

Motioning to Sue to follow him, Marcus set off towards the back of the store.

"Let's get ourselves coffee before the troops arrive. They aren't a bad bunch, but they are nosey, especially Joan and Aline, they will want your life story. Sonya may be a bit off with you as she was in for the job too, and Alice is just weird but you will get used to her. If you get stuck with anything, just ask me or Rosie. In fact, Rosie could run the store without me or Grant, as she's a great people's person and has a memory like a computer for customer's names and the appliances they have bought. She runs all the stock movement with Jeff, our warehouse man. He's a diamond and gets on with his job, and no back chat, unlike Robbie who was here before."

"Ah yes," Sue said, "I remember asking for stock once when we had a sale to complete and the person I spoke to was quite nasty and made me feel awkward. I assume that was him?"

"Yep that would be him. Not exactly Prince Charming," Marcus laughed.

"Who's not Prince Charming?" asked Joan Baxter as she stepped into the staff room.

Here we go, Marcus thought to himself, *it's Nosey Norah time already,* whilst replying to Joan, "Sue was just telling me she had rung for stock once and was surprised at how grumpy the person had been, needless to say it was Robbie."

"Ooh yes," Joan replied, "a right one he was! We were all scared to ask him for anything after that scrap he had with that lad from Newcastle, who came as holiday cover last year."

"I remember that incident very well, I was in the middle, and thank God Grant was in his office that day. He came down to help me separate them. Stick the kettle back on Marcus please," Rosie said as she entered the room and the conversation.

"So where's your partner in crime, Joan?" Marcus asked.

"We're not joined at the hip Marcus, she had to pop to the shop if you must know, and I don't see what business it is of yours, it's only 9.35 am now and we still have 10 minutes before TTT," Joan spat.

Rosie shot Marcus a look as he sighed, "Okay, Joan, let's not start the day on the wrong footing, I wasn't trying to be funny, it's just a cliché."

Sue was looking very uncomfortable at this point.

"I'm popping to the loo before TTT," and with this comment she went out the staff room door and was almost knocked off her feet by Aline, who was rushing in with a large bag of shopping.

"Oh sorry, you must be Sue, I'm Aline, must grab a coffee before TTT," she spluttered as she barged past and through the door.

Dear me, Sue thought to herself, making sure she had locked the loo door, *I guess that's trial by fire!*

After washing her hands and reapplying her lipstick, Sue went back into the tea-room. The atmosphere seemed to have calmed down and the other staff had arrived.

"Right," Marcus shouted as everyone was talking at once, "let's go to the signing up room and do TTT and get this show on the road."

They all filed out through the double doors and into the signing up room. As there were only six chairs, Marcus perched on the edge of one of the tables, with Sue standing next to him.

"So folks I want you to give a warm welcome to Sue, your new assistant manager. If Grant and I are off together anytime, then Sue will be in charge. We are very happy to have her on board as she has a wealth of knowledge on all fronts, as she has been working for the company for over five years–the same as most of us, as you may remember a lot of stores opened around that time."

Rosie remembered it well, as she had been the voice of It's Electric, going to three store openings as well as her own. The farthest had been Wakefield – what a long day that was!

Her job had been to meet and greet people and advertise the opening on the retail parks via a 'Madonna' type headset/mic which carried her voice through large speakers placed outside the stores. It was all good fun, with raffles, balloons, free sweets etc., and introduced the staff to potential customers of course. Rosie had loved that time.

Marcus noticed the faraway look in Rosie's eyes as he asked her for the print out of the day's figures.

"I will let Sue introduce herself properly first, then we can get up-to-speed with today's targets," Marcus said, shuffling the papers Rosie had handed to him.

Sue took a deep breath and started to speak, "Hello everyone, I'm Sue Goodall lately of Seaham store, which as Marcus said is where I have been part of the sales team for five years. I'm really looking forward to being here permanently and being able to help us achieve top store status, or at least be well up the ladder this year. I'm hoping to help everyone achieve their targets as I can see by the figures over the last few weeks what a great team you are. Any questions, feel free to ask me later as it's only five minutes to opening time. So, Marcus, back to you and today's targets."

"Right, everyone, yesterday was the start of a new week, targets are all the same as you usually have, you should know what they are by now. Rosie should have given you all your sales cards yesterday, for anyone who wasn't in-they are on the counter to be picked up. Go get 'em folks, and remember TTT," and with that he shooed them all out, with Jeff heading to the warehouse and Rosie heading behind the counter.

Marcus and Sue headed to the front of the shop into the meet and greet position.

"Grant should be in at 12 today," Marcus told Sue, "you won't meet Alice and Bob till the weekend as Alice is only weekend staff, and Bob has cut his hours as he is retiring next month. Bob won't need any help and is no bother, but Alice is a different kettle of fish. She does well against targets but Rosie and I both think her customers buy just to get away from her. She's like a limpet once she talks to anyone, and watch out for squabbling, if any of her customers come back and one of the others does the sale. Especially Joan and Aline, as it tends to turn into a regular cat fight. Oh and Sonya is due in at 2, she does a fine line in supercilious sniping."

Sue nodded and laughed, "So plenty to keep me on my toes then!"

Chapter 13

Rosie was standing behind the counter gazing across the shop floor, after she had made sure she had everyone's sales charts loaded onto the store system. Mondays were quiet, sales-wise usually, but often people started trying to cancel their purchases after getting a better deal in a competitor's store, but mostly they could price match or point out that it may not be exactly the same appliance and save the sale.

She had a good feeling about Sue, but also detected a hint of sadness about her for some reason. *Ah well, I better go and tackle the mountain of paperwork from the weekend.* So she called across to Marcus to let him know she was off to her office.

As she entered the warehouse, she saw Jeff disappearing into the small appliances store room behind her office at the far end of the building. God knows what the mess is like in there this morning, she was thinking to herself, as Jeff stepped out from the corridor leading to the back door, which made her jump!

"Sorry Rosie, I didn't mean to scare you," Jeff apologised.

"It's okay, Jeff," Rosie replied, saying nothing about the fact she thought she had seen him go into the stock room.

After all, she didn't want to scare him as he had to work in there.

She assumed the ghostly person tended to appear when changes were happening, as last time when both herself and Marcus had spotted him, it was just before all the trouble with Jason and when Jonathon was up to his old tricks adding insurance on to the customer's sales without their consent.

A vision of Mr Williams fabulous house and his wagging finger sprang into her mind. Still it all ended okay with Mr Williams, as his wife bought a top-of-the-range food mixer a couple of weeks later and specifically asked to be served by Rosie.

Seated behind her desk she started on the large pile of paper work. Around two hours later, Rosie had made good headway through the pile and probably could have it finished by the time it was her lunch hour.

Just then, her office door opened and Grant poked his head into the room.

"Hi Rosie, how's it going, you look like you've made a dent in that lot," he said pointing at the pile of papers. "Are they all winners, no mistakes or refunds going on?"

"No Grant," Rosie grinned at him, "it's all ship shape and Bristol fashion up to now and I only have about six to check. We have had a good start to the week thank goodness."

Sunday was the first day of the week at It's Electric, as all the previous week's figures were loaded onto the sales system on a Saturday night.

"Great stuff," Grant grinned back, "I'm going to be tied up taking Sue through procedures etc. for most of the day, if you and Marcus can hold the fort for me."

"Yep, no problem, Grant, I will finish these last few off, and have lunch, then go on the shop floor and let Marcus have his lunch then," Rosie replied.

Grant withdrew his head and popping his arm through instead, gave Rosie a thumbs up.

Rosie heard Sue's heels tapping up the metal staircase, then the low hum of conversation between her and Grant as she finished the last of her paperwork. She glanced at her watch, it was 1 pm so definitely lunch time. *Just two more boxes to check on this sheet then I can eat,* she thought, *I didn't realise how hungry I was till now.*

Entering the tea-room, she found Sonya Glass drinking a cup of coffee and leafing through the company quarterly magazine. She glanced up at Rosie and with a condescending look on her face she said, "I see Sue's promotion has a half page including a photo of her and David Smithson shaking her hand, must be nice to be appreciated eh? Did you or Grant alert the magazine then?"

"Neither of us did Sonya," Rosie answered over her shoulder as she reached into the fridge for her sandwich and yoghurt.

"I expect it was Seaham's manager George Gilbert, or maybe Smithson himself as he's into looking like the magnanimous friendly boss at the moment."

"So where is Suethen, cause she isn't on the shop floor," Sonya shot back.

"She's in the inner sanctum with Grant, Sonya, as they have lots of procedures to discuss, especially as this is a bigger store than Seaham. It will be a lot of hard work for her in the first few weeks, especially all that boring stuff one has to know. It nearly drove me crazy when I first became sales admin. Being in sales is so much easier." Rosie replied.

"Well, I'm not going to know any time soon, am I?" Sonya huffed.

"There will be other opportunities Sonya," Rosie sighed, "Believe me things can change on the turn of a sixpence. Look at me, there wasn't a sales admin post when I first started, that had enough hours to suit, but now it's changed."

Rosie's post was spread over five days, which fitted in with her children and her second job at the hotel behind the bar.

"I suppose," Sonya sniffed, as she squirted herself with perfume and left the staff room.

Blimey, I wish she wouldn't do that when I'm eating, now I have a cheese and coco channel sandwich, yuck, Rosie shuddered.

Looking at her watch, she realised her break time was up. *Right, it's up and at em again then*, she thought to herself, *and I must remind Grant to check people's holidays before he does the rota, as I'm sure he forgets, and I know Joan is going to her apartment in Majorca soon, as she never stops talking about it and her new soft furnishings, a regular Mrs Bucket,* Rosie laughed.

Holidays weren't something Rosie got a lot of. Mostly it was a Blackpool weekend to let off steam with a few close friends.

She went out onto the shop floor and behind the counter where Marcus was standing, she thought he looked tired today.

"Ah Rosie, it must be my lunch hour then."

"It most certainly is Marcus, you look like you could do with some fresh air," Rosie replied.

"Yeah, I feel a bit jaded to be honest," Marcus answered. "It's been a hard few weeks, but should ease off a bit for me now we have Sue on board. I think I will wander round to the supermarket and get something vaguely wholesome, my diet has been rubbish lately," he said as he headed for the door and out into the sunshine.

It's so nice out here, he thought, *I really need to organise myself. Some time off now Sue's here, I will have a look at the holiday calendar when I get back. It's probably going to have to be pretty soon as I know Grant will need to be off in August cause of the kids. Hmm, we're in the first week of June now, so maybe last week in June or first in July if I can get something booked last minute? That sounds like a good plan.* He felt his spirits lifting as he went into the supermarket.

Chapter 14

Grant and Sue had been ploughing through the procedures for over two hours, when Sue was aware of her tummy rumbling loudly!

"Ooops sorry Grant," she squeaked, more than a bit embarrassed.

"It's fine, don't worry about it and anyway it's a good signal telling us to stop and get lunch. It's just after 2 pm so no wonder your tummy's rumbling," Grant laughed. "Did you bring lunch or do I need to point you in the right direction for food?"

"I do need to go and get something as I didn't prep any lunch for today," Sue replied.

"Well there's a supermarket round the corner, it has a café too, or McDonalds which you probably saw on the way in, or there is a Greggs and a fish shop about five minutes' drive, down the road," Grant informed Sue.

"Supermarket I think for me, as I need a salad bowl or similar fresh food to pep me up. See you in an hour then Grant. Do you want me to go on the shop floor when I come back?" Sue asked.

"Yeah, good idea, Sue, I think we have had enough of procedures for one day," Grant answered raising his eyebrows.

After her lunch, Sue went onto the shop floor.

"Oh, hi Sue," Rosie called to her. "Do you want me to show you where everything is behind here as I'm due off at 4 pm."

"Yes Rosie that would be good, your back counter is twice the size of Seaham's and I see you have a lot more add on stock than we had," Sue answered, staring at all the bulbs, wires, scart leads and vacuum bags displayed on the wall.

"I try to top them up every day I'm in, as it's part of my job, but sometimes the stock supply doesn't run smoothly, to say the least, especially the vacuum bags. Customers get mighty annoyed if they bought the appliance here then can't get the bags, but there is a stall in Durham indoor market that keeps many more than us in stock, so I usually try to point them in that direction if they are desperate. All the stock systems are the same, apart from the fact when you log in–it's store 276 not 235."

"That's going to take me a while to remember," Sue laughed, "235 is almost a part of my DNA now, after five years of typing it in. Watch out for mistakes coming your way."

The pair spent another 30 minutes or so chatting, as the shop was quiet, exchanging bits of personal information as well as work based stuff.

Just as Sue had asked Rosie if it was true she was a psychic, as she had heard whispers on the grapevine, Joan and Aline approached the counter.

"I will tell you later," Rosie said quietly.

"Were off shift now Sue. No doubt we will see you tomorrow, we're on the graveyard shift, though why we bother coming in, I don't know, as we are never going to make target with those hours," Joan grumbled, with Aline nodding vigorously in agreement.

"I know it's quite often a quiet shift, as Grant has shown me figures, but my attitude is we never know whose coming through the door," Sue said gently.

"Huh, chance would be a fine thing," Joan said witheringly, as they went to get their coats and bags.

As they walked off, Rosie sighed and said to Sue, "Good luck with those two, they are a pair of grumps at the best of times, but on a graveyard shift they are two positive rays of sunshine, altogether."

"Don't worry Rosie, we had a grumpy contingent at Seaham too, though it was only one and a bloke." Sue laughed.

"See you tomorrow, Sue," Rosie replied, as she went off to get her bag and coat too.

A few minutes later, Rosie left the store waving to the others as she went.

Grant appeared on the shop floor as Marcus was about to go off shift.

"Hi Sue," Grant said, "as Marcus is away home now, I will be down here with you, we never have just one member of management on the shop floor here, unlike some of the smaller stores, but you will be in charge of sales, not me."

"Okay," Sue answered, "no problem."

The rest of the day passed without any problems, but unfortunately, it passed without any sales. Grant watched Sue shutting the sales system down.

"Right, that's us then Grant," Sue said.

"I hope today wasn't too boring Sue," Grant answered as he held the door open to the warehouse. "We have done most of the procedure stuff now, so another couple of hours and you should be up to speed."

"Yeah it's boring stuff I have to admit," said Sue shrugging into her coat, "but needs must eh?"

"Have you got everything?" Grant asked as they left the store.

"Yep I have, and if I haven't, I know where it is," Sue laughed, heading to her car with a cheery wave.

Chapter 15

Rosie watched Sue expertly parking her Fiat 500 the following morning.

"How did the rest of yesterday go then Sue?" Rosie inquired.

"Not bad," Sue replied. "I just hope I can get these doors open and the fob is working, we only had a push up shutter at Seaham and ordinary doors."

"Just point it at that square on the side and it should go up," Rosie replied, "that's it, now we just have to pull the sliding doors open a bit and we should be in. Don't let the shutter go all the way up though, we need to duck down to get in, or the customers will be walking in before we are open."

"Crikey I had forgotten how dark it is in here!" Sue gasped.

Just then a shaft of light appeared, "Don't worry I have this tiny torch on my key ring, it's just enough to see the light switches on the wall. I got it free when we did some appliance training with Hitachi a bit back." Rosie smiled at Sue.

Sue spotted the switches and the lights sprang to life with their usual pinging noise when first switched on. As they made their way towards the double doors leading to the warehouse, Rosie asked Sue if Sonya had been okay with her after she had gone.

"She was okay but slightly prickly," Sue revealed. "I can't blame her really, as I would probably have felt the same if the shoe was on the other foot, and it was me who didn't get the job. Especially in her own store."

"True," Rosie agreed, "it must be a bit disappointing."

After TTT that morning, Rosie retreated to her office as there was paperwork to attend to.

Sifting through the sales invoices and loading them onto the system, she could see as a shop they were second topping the region, but she could also see that Joan and Aline were at the bottom in the store and only fourth from bottom in the region. She knew in her bones that David Smithson would be giving Grant earache over that, as everyone has to be bottom some time, but not all the time. *I hope Sue can shake them up*, she thought, but knowing the gruesome twosome she doubted it very much.

A short while later, she heard footsteps on the stairs. There was a brief knock and Sue came into the office.

"Hi Rosie, any chance you could look over this sales pitch I've written and see if it makes sense to you?" she asked.

"Yeah sure," Rosie replied. "Do you want me to do it now, or should I pop down when I'm finished here?"

"Just bring it down, there's no rush," Sue replied, "see you shortly."

Once Rosie finished the invoices she sat back and perused Sue's work.

Looks good to me, she ruminated. *If I'm honest we could all do with some refresher training, including me. It's over a year for me and I know I forget the tricks of the trade as I'm not doing actual sales very often now.*

Rosie finished off the last of the paperwork, and went down to the shop floor.

Sue and Marcus were standing in the meet and greet position at the front of the store.

"That looks great Sue," Rosie called out, as she walked towards them.

Sue answered with a smile, "I've just been telling Marcus, he thinks we should do it every six months as a refresher."

"I agree," said Rosie, "because I have forgotten half of what I originally learnt. You're looking very pleased with yourself today, Marcus, care to let us in on the secret?"

Marcus's face split into a wide grin. "I'm going on holiday in two weeks' time to Faliraki in Rhodes. I got a really cheap deal for a single self-catering apartment as it's a last-minute booking. I popped into the travel agents to pick up some brochures, but they were putting up deals in the window when I got there, so I asked if there was anything for single travellers and the girl came up with this. So I rang Grant and asked if I could book the time off and he said yes. Because it was so cheap, I booked it there and then. I can't wait to go."

"I love Rhodes," Rosie breathed. "It was my first ever holiday abroad, but in Rhodes town itself, not Faliraki. The old town is very beautiful, you must try to get to see it. I will eventually go back, but not till the kids have left home as I'm a real cultural history geek, and the kids would be bored stiff with my preferred type of holiday."

"Well I'm not really the clubbing type so as long as there's a bar close by, that will do for me," Marcus replied.

"I'm off shortly," Rosie told Marcus, "as I'm covering in the hotel for a couple of hours, as the boss needs to go out, so it will be short and sweet just like me," she laughed, "so I better go and get my stuff," and she walked back up to the double doors.

"I don't know how she does it," Marcus marvelled as he watched her retreating figure, "she's got two teenagers and a four-year-old, is a single parent, and works two jobs and often looks really tired, but she always has a smile on her face."

"Yep," Sue agreed, "she seems like a nice person. She's certainly helped me over the last two days. How she puts up with Joan and Aline, I don't know."

"Speak of the devil and so she appears," Marcus nodded towards Joan's arc which had just pulled in. "The gruesome twosome. Incidentally, our Rosie has tendency to give people nick names, and that's one of hers for these two."

A short while later, Joan and Aline were on the shop floor discussing her apartment in Majorca as usual, as her holidays were approaching.

Deeply engrossed in their conversation, neither of them noticed Marcus till he said, "Right we need some sales on tonight or Grant's going to be on the warpath."

"He can be whatever he likes, if there's no customers what does he expect us to do!" Joan spat. "We haven't got a magic wand, have we?"

"No, we definitely don't," Aline agreed.

At this point, Sue joined the group and said, "I understand you not liking the graveyard shift, as it's often quiet, but it's a good time to spruce up your sections and do stock checking, plus reading up on new appliances we have, so you are ready with any info that customers want. In fact, starting next week,

Dave is going to be doing in-house-training on the brown goods so you all know how to sell TVs, videos and hi-fis. I know you both find it difficult to sell them looking at your sales figures. A few Brown sales would boost your sales against target. You would reap the benefits of extra Commission Girls, and it would keep David Smithson from wanting to transfer people."

Joan's face said it all.

"Transfer people. What do you mean, I'm going nowhere, if he tries to transfer me, I will just leave or get the union involved!"

Aline went as white as a sheet!

"How can I get here? Joan and I car share as I haven't got transport. I would have to go on the dole! Oh my god my Barry will go bananas if my wage stops!"

"Look girls, the whole reason behind training and us selling better to whoever comes in, is to stop that situation occurring. I'm sure between us we can do this."

"Well let's hope so, come on Aline, let's go and get some cleaning stuff, at least it's something to pass the time," Joan huffed.

Sue watched them go into the warehouse, she sighed deeply, rubbing her forehead and said to Marcus, "Now I know exactly what Rosie meant about those two."

Chapter 16

Joan and Aline are off today, thank goodness, Rosie thought to herself, *but it's Sonya's long shift today and she seemed strangely quiet at TTT this morning. Oh well, I'm sure Sue can cope with the likes of her. The delivery should be here soon, I better check with Jeff to make sure he's okay.*

She went down to the warehouse where Jeff was making room for the new stock coming in. She knew some of the TVs and videos had been sold with installation, so they would be picked up by Alex, the TV installation guy in the morning. He came up from regional office, in Bradford every Thursday, to do the installs in their area. Rosie often wondered how he coped with so much driving, especially on Fridays as he had to go to the Newcastle and Cramlington stores, which were much further afield! It was at least a two-hour drive before even starting to find customer's houses.

Just then there was a loud banging on the door.

"That's the van now Jeff, I will go and get Dave to give you a hand." Rosie dashed off onto the shop floor and found Dave in the brown goods section readjusting the TVs and tuning in the new ones as usual.

"Hi Dave, do you fancy giving Jeff a hand with the delivery?" she asked.

"Yeah of course, happy to help," Dave answered, heading to the warehouse.

They are no bother those two, Rosie thought to herself, *unlike the gruesome twosome.*

As Rosie went out onto the shop floor, she noticed Sonya talking to Sue. *Hmm, I bet Sonya's giving her the third degree* she thought as she approached them.

Sure enough she heard Sonya asking Sue did her husband not mind her being a career woman.

"No Eddie is always happy to let me do what I think is important to me," Rosie heard Sue reply as she joined the pair.

"Hi Rosie," Sue smiled at her, "was that the delivery van I saw going past?"

"Yeah, Sue it arrived about five minutes ago. Dave is helping Jeff with the unloading," Rosie replied.

"Ah, okay, in that case, Sonya can you cover the brown goods section while Dave is busy, I will go to the meet and greet, and Rosie could you stay here amongst the washers? I hear you're quite the expert. Marcus told me you were head hunted by Siemens and worked in a competitor's store in Newcastle for a while selling washers," Sue said.

"Yeah, I did for a while, I'm happy in the white goods. All those TVs with all the wires, handsets and gizmos attached just make me feel confused," Rosie laughed, crossing her eyes for good measure.

An hour later, Dave came back onto the shop floor.

Sonya came over to Rosie and said, "You can go behind the counter now if you like."

"Good idea," Rosie replied, "I can get on filling up the add on stock now the delivery has arrived."

"So do you think she's going to be up to the job then?" Sonya asked.

"You mean Sue?" Rosie enquired, "my mother always used to say, whose she the cat's mother?"

"What do you mean?" Sonya said crossly.

"It refers to being disrespectful, not calling the person by their name. That's old school manners for you I guess," shrugged Rosie. "And yes, I think Sue's going to be really good. She has some great ideas I think, and it's time the boys got a run for their money. Plus, David Smithson is up for promoting women at the moment, as a new female manager is starting at one of the southern stores next week I've heard on the grape vine. He doesn't do being second in anything, so as I tried to tell you before, things can change on a sixpence, so your chance could come again, Sonya."

"What great ideas," Sonya asked, looking slightly less peeved, as what Rosie had said sank in.

"That's up to Sue to tell everyone at TTT when the whole team are in, so sorry I can't say at the moment," Rosie replied, "I'm going to fill up the add on, so catch you later."

Sonya looked at Rosie's retreating back feeling thoroughly disgruntled. *Next time a post comes up in another shop I'm out of here, then maybe Grant will appreciate my skills* she pondered, letting her miffed thoughts run riot for the next few minutes, till she realised Sue was directing a customer towards her.

The next couple of days went past quite smoothly. Sue was finding her feet and Marcus was feeling much happier now he knew that the store wouldn't be a shambles when he went on holiday, with poor Rosie stressed to the max, trying to keep things going, which is what used to happen previously, when Jason Doubleday was left in charge.

Chapter 17

Sue woke early on Saturday morning. Having had a day off on Friday, she was feeling reinvigorated.

She dropped a kiss on Eddie's head, stretched, got up and headed to the bathroom.

Stepping out of the shower, breathing in the smell of her citrus body wash, Sue looked at herself in the mirror, and said out loud, "I can do this, bring it on."

Today was the day the full staff team would be in, including Alice whom everyone said was a bit odd to say the least. *So the dynamic should be interesting,* she thought, as so far, she had only met them in dribs and drabs.

Fifteen minutes later, she was ready and dashed down to the kitchen to grab a bowl of cereal and a coffee. Eddie handed her a lunch box with crisps, sandwiches and a yoghurt in.

"It's just plain ham in the sarnies pet, I will do the shopping later on, and do you fancy Chinese tonight and a bottle of wine? You might need a drink after today, love," he said laughing.

"Sounds good to me," she replied, swallowing a mouthful of coffee, "I must dash."

Eddie slid her car keys across the breakfast bar, which she grabbed, quickly giving him a peck as she put her jacket on and hurried out.

Marcus was already there when she arrived, "Morning Sue," he said smiling clicking his fob to raise the metal shutters. "Ready for this and your first meeting with the full team?"

"As ready as I will ever be," she said, as they slid the electric doors back and ducked under the partly open shutters.

"Let's grab a coffee before the Mongol hoards descend as Rosie would say," Marcus laughed, "that's assuming there's milk as Rosie was off yesterday and mostly it's her who remembers to buy it, the others just use it!"

Luckily Rosie, as usual thinking ahead, had bought two lots of four pints of milk on her way in , so there was still one carton left when Marcus opened the fridge.

He grabbed two cups and made the coffee.

"Is there enough water in the kettle for me?" Rosie asked, as she shucked her way out of her raincoat on the way into the staff room.

"Yes, there sure is, I will make one for you," Marcus replied.

"I'm just in time," Rosie said, sipping the scalding coffee gratefully, "the others were all pulling off the main road and into the retail park as I came in."

As she finished speaking, the door opened, and everyone came in at once, making a beeline for the kettle.

Grant was the only one missing as he usually arrived just in time for TTT.

"Sue should you and I go on the shop floor?" Marcus suggested, trying to squeeze past everyone to get out.

"Yep, I'm with you Marcus," Sue replied, clutching her cup and following him out.

"So is that her then?" Alice asked in an undertone, sidling up to Rosie.

"Well it's not the queen mother is it," Joan sniggered.

A dark cloud descended over Alice's face.

"Now ladies let's not start the day on the wrong footing," Rosie advised, "get your cups and let's go to the signing up room, no good hanging about in here, it's nearly TTT time."

Dave held the door open as they all filed out, and as Bob went past, he rolled his eyes at Dave signalling what kind of day he thought it might be.

"Good grief Sonya," Dave spluttered as she went past, "Did you have a bath in that perfume this morning, it's taking my breath away."

She gave him a look of absolute disgust. "It's called Angel and I think it's fabulous. It's no 1 on men's most liked perfumes for women, so I don't know what's wrong with your sense of smell," she threw at him.

"Angel? I will be with the angels if I breath any more of that in pet, blimey," Dave replied, shaking his head and coughing into a handkerchief.

Rosie overheard the exchange as she had run upstairs to her office and was just coming back down. *Oh no,* she sighed to herself, *there's another one full of the joys of spring now and we aren't even open yet!*

Everyone was in the signing up room and ready for TTT by 9.45 am.

"Okay, folks," Marcus shouted over the hubbub of everyone still talking, "let's get on with TTT. I think everyone has met Sue but Bob and Alice, is that right?"

There was a general sound of agreement.

"So Sue is going to run TTT this morning, aren't you Sue?"

"Yes, I am," Sue said stepping forward, "So hi folks, in the last few days, I've been going through everyone's sales figures and as a team I think we could all do with a refresher on sales training. So, to start with, can you all fill in the questionnaire which I'm going to hand out, as I want to know your thoughts and what you would want to gain from a refresher course. Most of you have been with the company a fair few years now and I know myself that I sometimes just go through the motions when I'm selling instead of really engaging with the customer. Once you have done that, I will set up our own in-store-training pack, that we can do together at TTT on a Saturday morning, or at any time when it's quiet. If any of you have any ideas you want me to implement, just let me know. I'm handing you back to Marcus now to do the targets for today, while I hand out the questionnaires to you all."

Just then Grant appeared at the door saying, "Morning troops, ready for the fray then everyone? Let's hope this is a busy one and TTT."

With a cheery wave, he headed into the warehouse.

Marcus read out the shop's target for the day, and everyone's individual targets and they exited the signing up room clutching their questionnaires.

Rosie was behind the counter, ready to put any sales through, while Sue and Marcus had moved to the meet and greet position at the front of the store.

The others were in a huddle in the middle amongst the washers and chest freezers.

Rosie eyed the group as they knew they weren't meant to stand together, but they were obviously discussing the questionnaire, as Joan was waving hers about imperiously.

Hmm, I think Sue may get a few questions fired at her, looking at Joan's reaction Rosie thought to herself. *I'm glad it's my Sunday off this week.*

Alongside the paper waving, Joan was also holding forth. "So what do you all think about this then? I don't need any more training, I've been in retail for 25 years this year, what can she teach me that I don't already know?"

"Yes, Joan, I agree," affirmed Aline, "It's 20 years for me. Teaching her granny to suck eggs I think."

Sonya chewed her lip a little then said, "I can see why she wants to do it, cause really our figures haven't been great lately as you must have realised. We missed the shop's target last month and Grant's face has been tripping him up since Jonathon went."

"Oh yes, him with his dodgy deals were really impressive, have you seen some of the juggling and crawling to customers Grant has had Rosie do to save the sales after some of his mega deals?"

"You're right, Joan, but you and Aline really need to get up to speed with the new TVs etc., after all a top-end Toshiba or Hitachi with surround sound would give you a good boost in just one sale," Sonya said.

"That's all well and good," Joan replied, "but I don't understand all that high-tech stuff."

"And neither do I," Aline agreed.

All this time Alice hadn't said a word and was just standing staring at Aline, who suddenly realised Alice was looking at her.

"Why are you staring at me like that Alice?" she asked.

"Well did she then, your granny?" Alice said.

Aline, looking very perplexed, was now staring at Alice, "What are you talking about Alice?" she sighed.

"The eggs, did your granny suck the eggs? I've lived on a farm all my life and my granny didn't suck any eggs that I know of," Aline looked at Alice and shook her head.

"It's a saying Alice, no one's granny actually sucked eggs."

"So why did you say it then?" Alice queried.

Sonya was literally rolling about laughing by this time.

Joan rolled her eyes, looking up to the ceiling, "For Christ's sake Alice, you can't be serious," she said, "I've heard it all now. Anyway, Marcus is heading this way so we better split up," she said moving off to the small appliances.

"Right ladies, what's going on and Alice why are you looking so confused?" Marcus asked.

"It's the eggs and her granny," Alice answered, nodding towards Aline.

It was Marcus's turn to look confused.

"What eggs?" he queried.

Sonya let out a huge guffaw and walked off giggling.

"Look this isn't a time for silly conversations, here come some customers, so let's get our business heads on, please," Marcus said. "Alice if you're confused about something go and ask Rosie, she's usually really good at straightening stuff out."

Rosie watched Alice approaching the counter and braced herself as the look Alice had on her face said it all.

"Marcus says I have to ask you about the eggs Rosie."

"Eggs, Alice? What eggs?" Rosie questioned.

"The ones Aline's granny sucked," Alice replied.

It was Rosie's turn to look confused.

Luckily at this point, Aline came up to the counter with a sale.

"I will put you out of your misery Rosie, I was complaining about the training Sue is going to do and said it was like teaching your granny to suck eggs. This one actually thinks my granny did suck eggs and completely missed the point as per usual," Aline said to Rosie passing her the details of the kettle she was selling.

"Ah, I see," Rosie replied, trying not to laugh.

"Alice, it's a saying which means that Aline feels it's pointless doing more training when she has been selling for years."

"Well, why didn't she just say that then," Alice replied, stomping off in a huff.

Aline shook her head at Rosie and went off to get the customer's purchase from the warehouse.

I really don't know how Alice manages to bring up kids and help on the farm as well as doing this when her brain seems to be full of cotton wool, Rosie laughed to herself.

The rest of the day went quite smoothly with a few big sales nabbed by Sonya and one for Joan and Aline both made their targets by Sue handing them some of her sales as she didn't have a target nor get commission as management, so it made sense to her to let the team benefit instead.

Grant was full of smiles at closing time as the shop had made target too, and all the tills balanced and the stock was right.

"Well done everyone, what a great day. See what happens when we all pull together," he enthused, "and well done to you Sue for a stirling first week. Marcus and I really appreciate all your hard work and can't wait to see the outcome when your training module starts. Could be a feather in our cap with David Smithson."

"Yes," Marcus said, "I couldn't agree more Sue, it's certainly took a weight off my shoulders, you being part of the team."

"So that's it folks and see you all tomorrow. Rosie I know it's your Sunday off so I will see you on Monday. Let's see if we can start the week as positively as we have ended this one." Grant said happily.

For once, no one was moaning as they left and got into their cars.

Marcus switched the lights off, stepped out of the sliding doors and clicked his fob to lower the shutters.

One more week, he smiled to himself, *and it will be sun, sea and cocktails for me, thank God,* as he hopped into his car and drove away from It's Electric.